W9-AMN-637

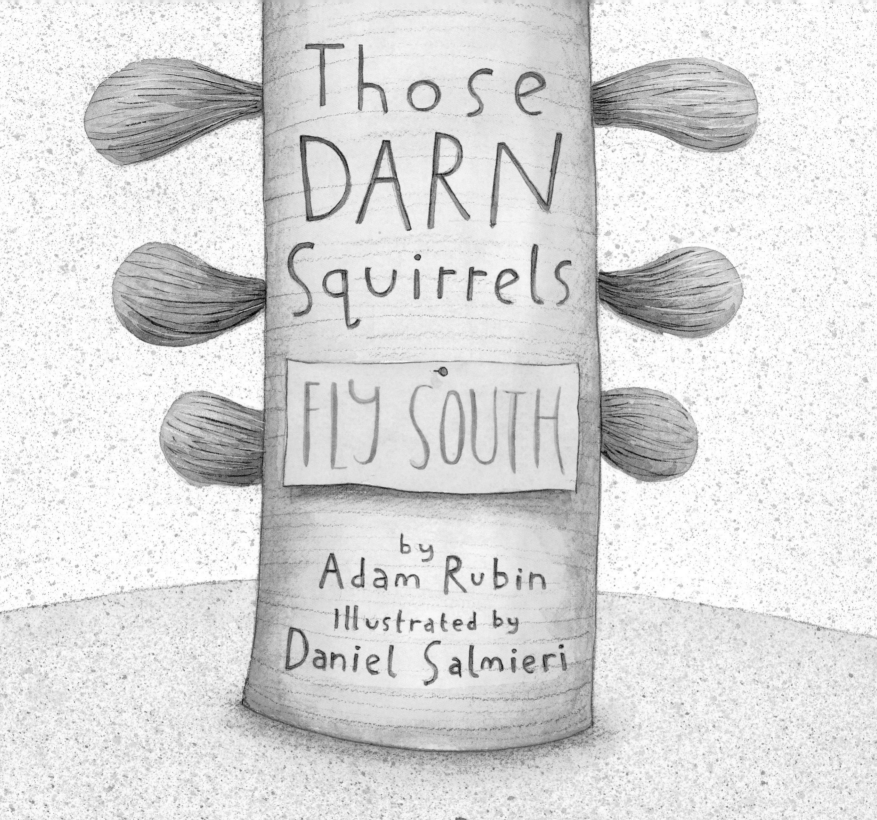

Those DARN Squirrels

FLY SOUTH

by
Adam Rubin

Illustrated by
Daniel Salmieri

Clarion Books
Houghton Mifflin Harcourt · Boston New York 2012

Clarion Books
215 Park Avenue South
New York, New York 10003

Text copyright © 2012 by Adam Rubin
Illustrations copyright © 2012 by Daniel Salmieri

All rights reserved.

For information about permission to reproduce selections from this book,
write to Permissions, Houghton Mifflin Harcourt Publishing Company,
215 Park Avenue South, New York, New York 10003.

Clarion Books is an imprint of Houghton Mifflin Harcourt Publishing Company.

www.hmhbooks.com

The illustrations were executed in watercolor, gouache, and colored pencil.
The text was set in 16-point Jacoby ICG Light.
Book design by Kerry Martin

Library of Congress Cataloging-in-Publication Data
Rubin, Adam, 1983–
Those darn squirrels fly south / by Adam Rubin ; illustrated by Daniel Salmieri.
p. cm.
Summary: As Old Man Fookwire's birds prepare to migrate south for the winter, those darn squirrels decide to follow.
ISBN 978-0-547-67823-8 (hardcover)
[1. Squirrels—Fiction. 2. Birds—Fiction. 3. Human-animal relationships—Fiction. 4. Old age—Fiction.
5. Humorous stories.] I. Salmieri, Daniel, 1983–ill. II. Title.
PZ7.R83116Tim 2012
[E]—dc23
2011041584

Manufactured in Singapore

TWP 10 9 8 7 6 5 4 3 2 1

4500354660

For my loving grandparents—
Nana and Papa flew south for the winter,
Grandma and Grandpa do headstands for fun.
—A.R.

For Sean and Arianne
—D.S.

JAN 1 2 2013

OLD Man Fookwire lived at the edge of town in a beautiful forest full of birds and squirrels. But he was such a grump! He scolded fireflies for being too bright. He yelled at clouds for being too fluffy. And when the lilacs bloomed, he pinched his nose with a clothespin so he wouldn't have to smell their scent.

Even for a grump like Fookwire, it had been a glorious summer. He'd spent most of his time painting the colorful birds that visited his backyard. Sometimes, by accident, he painted a squirrel. Other times, the squirrels painted themselves. Then Fookwire would shake his old-man fist and shout, "Those darn squirrels!"

Dear Diary,
The Birds are going to leave soon and that makes me sad.

But now it was fall. The weather had turned crisp, the leaves had changed colors, and soon the birds would fly south for the winter. Fookwire would have to endure the long, cold winter months alone.

Well, not exactly alone. The squirrels would be there, too.

Normally, the squirrels spent winters playing Ping-Pong, building ships in bottles, and knitting. But this year they had other plans. They were curious about where the birds went for winter vacation. So they'd decided to follow them.

Now, not many people know this, but squirrels have a comprehensive understanding of aerodynamic engineering. They built gyro-copters from pinecones. They built gliders from leaves. They even built a zeppelin from an old shopping bag.

When the first frost arrived, the bonga birds took off, followed by the baba birds and the yaba birds. They circled the house, waved goodbye to Fookwire, and headed south. The floogle bird spent a few minutes scarfing up the last of the farfle seeds. Then he took off, too.

Fookwire pouted as the sound of flapping wings faded into the distance. He turned to go inside— and heard a rustling in the trees. A rustling followed by a whir. A whir followed by a buzz.

It was the squirrels, launching their flying machines one by one. Some of the aircraft flew straighter than others. But eventually, they all flew up, up, and away from the harvest-colored treetops and into the cool blue autumn air.

The old man could hardly believe his eyes. "Great googley-moogley!" he said. "It's a whole flock of flying squirrels!"

The squirrels followed the floogle bird for days.

They flew through the night.

They flew through the rain.

They even flew through turbulence.

Finally, just when the squirrels thought they
couldn't fly any longer, the floogle bird swooped
down and landed gracefully on a beach.
The squirrels landed with a crunch.

The beach was so warm and beautiful, and the squirrels were so happy to be done flying, they decided to have a fiesta. They went swimming and ate mangoes with salt and lime. They played the marimba and danced the merengue. The party lasted all night long.

Over the next few weeks, the squirrels made themselves right at home. There were many new plants to snack on. There were also many new birds to see. There were coco birds, kiki birds, and caramba birds . . . There were too many birds to count!

One of the birds reminded the squirrels of someone they knew.

Deep in the snowy woods, a strange noise woke old man Fookwire from his nap. It was coming from the telephone—he was getting a call! When he picked up the receiver, the operator asked if he would accept the charges for a long-distance call from the village of Santa Vaca. Then there was a chattering on the line.

"Those darn squirrels!" shouted Fookwire.

The old man missed the birds. And even though he would never admit it, he missed the squirrels, too. So he decided to join them.

Fookwire had a car that he kept under a tarp in a shed by the stream. He'd bought it in 1957 and had driven it only twice.

He loaded it up with his easel, paints, and brushes, fixed himself a snack of cottage cheese with pepper, and hit the road. Then he drove twelve miles an hour all the way to Santa Vaca.

The nice people behind him had plenty of time to admire his car.

Finally, Fookwire arrived in the little village. He spotted the floogle bird flying overhead and followed him to the beach. When he got out of the car, the squirrels gave him a big hug.

Maybe it was the nice weather. Maybe it was the beautiful scenery. Maybe it was the squirrels dancing in his pants. But for the first time in a very long time, the old man laughed.

Soon, Fookwire set up his easel and began to paint the local birds.

"Da-ba-dobo!" sang the coco bird.

"Ba-da-bobo!" sang the kiki bird.

Fookwire was overjoyed. "The birds here are even more amazing than the birds back home!" he exclaimed.

"Harrumph!" muttered the floogle bird.

The sun was very hot. Fookwire sweated, but he kept on painting.

Fookwire sweltered, but he kept on painting.

Then Fookwire slumped forward, face first, into his painting.

The squirrels dragged the old man into the shade and
gave him some water. He was as red as a bonga bird!

He decided it was time to go home. The squirrels decided to go with him. They'd had a wonderful vacation. But after all, it was almost time for their annual snow-fort building competition. They had one last snack of mango, then Fookwire waved goodbye to the birds, and they all piled into the car.